The Best Costumes Ever!

by Liza Charlesworth
illustrated by Claudio Cerri

ISBN: 979-8-225-02082-8

Publisher: Tara Welty
Creative Director: Tannaz Fassihi; Designer: Cynthia Ng

1 2 3 4 5 6 7 8 9 10 68 34 33 32 31 30 29 28 27 26 25

Made in Jiaxing City, China. First printing, August 2025.

SCHOLASTIC

It's time to read a tale about a sweet green monster named Frankenfran. Frankenfran had a snug home at the tippy top of a tall grassy peak. She baked cupcakes with her dad. She painted pictures with her mom. She hung out with her pet bat, Max.

Frankenfran had a perfect life except for one thing: She felt a little bit lonely. Each night, she sat in her dark room and stared out the window at the town below. The name of the town was Joyland and it was full of creatures called humans.

The humans seemed quite interesting!
They walked around and rode on bikes.
They played fun games and ate ice cream.
Frankenfran really wanted to meet them.
But how? She was a green monster and
they might be afraid of her.

Then Frankenfran had a brainstorm.
Tomorrow would be Halloween!
On her computer, she found out that
humans like to dress in spooky costumes
on that day. They might be a witch or a goblin.
They might be a ghost or a monster.

On Halloween, Frankenfran could go to Joyland without scaring a single human. Why? Because they would not know that she was a real monster. They would think she was just a kid in a very cool costume!

Frankenfran was thrilled with her plan! The next day at 3:00 sharp, she told her parents she was going out for a long walk. It was not a lie. She did, in fact, walk all the way down from the grassy peak until she reached the town of Joyland.

Was there a lot to see? Yes, indeed!
Frankenfran shook with excitement.
"Jeepers creepers!" she exclaimed.
She saw craggy trees and spider webs
and bright pumpkins with funny faces.

Best of all, Frankenfran saw a lot of spooky costumes! She saw a vampire! She saw a witch with a crooked hat. She saw a tall and slinky skeleton. She saw a mummy and a scarecrow and all sorts of amazing monsters.

Did Frankenfran blend in? You bet!
In fact, she made a new pal in a flash.
As she stood gawking, a ghost grabbed
her hand and said, “I like your costume.
Do you want to trick-or-treat with me?”
“Yes, please!” she replied with glee.

The two new pals dashed from home to
home, collecting lots of sweet treats.
DING, DONG! They got mints and bubble gum.
They got gumdrops and swirly lollipops.
They even got whole chocolate bars. Yum!
And every place they went, the humans said,
"Wow! You two have the best costumes ever."

After a while, their bags were brimming
with more sweets than they could eat.
It was then that the ghost whispered,
"Pssssssst. There is a costume contest
in the park. Let's both compete in it."
Did Frankenfran like that plan? She did!

Quick as a wink, the pals went to the park and hopped on stage to join the contest. They strutted. They turned and posed. Did one of them win first prize? Nope. The judge said: "I can't decide which of you has the best costume—so you BOTH win!"

After that, they sat on a bench to chat.
"I had such a good time!" said the ghost.
"Me, too," said Frankenfran with a smile.
"But it is time for me to tell you the truth.
You see, I am NOT a human in a costume.
I'm a real monster and my home is up there."
She pointed to the tall grassy peak.

Did the ghost shake and quake in fear?
Not a bit. He just smiled and replied,
"That makes me quite happy. You see,
I'm a real ghost and my home is up there."
He pointed to the tall snowy peak that
was right beside the tall grassy peak.
"Just like you, I came down here to enjoy
Halloween with the humans," he added.

"Gee, that is fantastic!" cried Frankenfran. "It feels so neat to have a real spooky pal. We can have fun play dates. You can visit my grassy peak and I can visit your snowy peak."

"Yes, indeed," replied the ghost. "And we can both meet in Joyland every Halloween!"